To C, my Bee
A.B.

To JM, the slowcoach I know
L.M.

First published 1998 by Walker Books Ltd
87 Vauxhall Walk, London SE11 5HJ

This edition published 1999

2 4 6 8 10 9 7 5 3

Text © 1998 Alison Boyle
Illustrations © 1998 Lydia Monks

This book has been typeset in Gill Sans Bold Educational.

Printed in Hong Kong

British Library Cataloguing in Publication Data
A catalogue record for this book is
available from the British Library.

ISBN 0-7445-6972-9

THIS WALKER BOOK BELONGS TO:

_____

_____

_____

_____

WHO GOES BUZZ?

A Spot-the-Difference Game Book

Alison Boyle   illustrated by Lydia Monks

WALKER BOOKS
AND SUBSIDIARIES
LONDON · BOSTON · SYDNEY

One day, Bee buzzed up to his friend Beetle.

Hi, Beetle! Want to buzz around the farm with me?

Yes please, Bee, but don't go too fast.

But buzz! went Bee.
He was gone.

Oh, Bee, wait for me!

Bee buzzed around the farmyard.

Look, Beetle.
See the cockerel?

But the cockerel has gone.
What four other things have gone?

What cockerel?
Oh, Bee, wait
for me!

Bee buzzed around the field.

Look, Beetle.
See the
black lamb?

But the black lamb has gone.
What four other things have gone?

Bee buzzed around the sty.

But the pig has gone. What four other things have gone?

What pig? Oh, Bee, wait for me!

Bee buzzed around the barn.

But the donkey has gone.
What four other things have gone?

Bee buzzed around the milking shed.

But the cow has gone.
What four other things have gone?

At the end of the day,
Bee felt tired.

Look, Beetle.
The stars
are out.

There are wild animals out, too.
Can you see them?

On their way home, Beetle and
Bee saw all the farm animals.

Can you see all the animals?

MORE WALKER PAPERBACKS
For You to Enjoy

Each book is on a different mathematical theme.
How many have you got?

WHERE IS LITTLE CROC?

Little Croc's not ready for his bath; he wants to play hide-and-seek with Mum.
He hides in lots of different rooms around the house.
Can you spot him and his toys?

0-7445-6971-0   £2.99

WHOSE HAT IS THAT?

Silly Cat has a red woolly hat; Ant has a blue hard hat. Bird, Giraffe, Snake,
Hippo and Elephant all have hats too. Can you help Silly Cat and Ant find their way
through the different mazes to meet each hatted friend?

0-7445-6973-7   £2.99

WHO GOES BUZZ?

Bee buzzes around the farm pointing out things for his friend,
Beetle, to see. But Beetle can't keep up and the scenes have changed by
the time he arrives! Can you spot the differences?

0-7445-6972-9   £2.99

WHAT GOES SNAP?

Penguin and Squeaky have lost some of their Snap cards so they decide to make
some new ones. They find things that match the pictures on the cards and, each time,
Penguin takes a photo. Can you spot the matching things?

0-7445-6974-5   £2.99

Walker Paperbacks are available from most booksellers, or by post from B.B.C.S., P.O. Box 941, Hull, North Humberside HU1 3YQ
24 hour telephone credit card line 01482 224626

To order, send: Title, author, ISBN number and price for each book ordered, your full name and address,
cheque or postal order payable to BBCS for the total amount and allow the following for postage and packing:
UK and BFPO: £1.00 for the first book, and 50p for each additional book to a maximum of £3.50.
Overseas and Eire: £2.00 for the first book, £1.00 for the second and 50p for each additional book.

Prices and availability are subject to change without notice.